STAND BACK, DON'T FEAR THE CHANGE

✺

STAND BACK, DON'T FEAR THE CHANGE

✻

NICK ADMUSSEN

NEW MICHIGAN PRESS

TUCSON, ARIZONA

NEW MICHIGAN PRESS

DEPT OF ENGLISH, P. O. BOX 210067

UNIVERSITY OF ARIZONA

TUCSON, AZ 85721-0067

<http://newmichiganpress.com>

Orders and queries to <nmp@thediagram.com>.

ISBN 978-1-934832-70-7. FIRST PRINTING.

Printed in the United States of America.

Design by Ander Monson.

Cover image: "Monkey Gaze" by Vincent G Chong
IG: @crystalmonkeycalligraphy
website: WWW.VINCENTCHONG.ART

CONTENTS

PARABLE OF THE NORTH TRAIN

The sleeper cars of trains have twelve compartments of six bunks apiece; the bunks are stacked three tall to the ceiling of the train and face each other across a three-foot aisle. In the left lower berth of the third compartment of the seventh car of a train headed north, an eighty-year old man stopped breathing and died. His wife, three feet across from him in the right lower berth, heard this, leaned over towards him, said "the bottled water delivery man is twenty-five minutes late!" and he awoke with a start.

The man in the left middle berth thought that if he had a little drink now, right after dinner, it would have a negligible effect on him and he'd still enjoy the magazine he had brought along to entertain himself. Then, when he finished the magazine, it would be late enough and he'd be tired and wouldn't want another drink. The woman in the right middle berth slept fitfully and dreamed she was putting her face into the exhibit at the science museum that was a bed of pins so close together that you couldn't prick yourself with them, and if you pressed your hand into it you could see its 3D outline. The metal felt like water on her closed eyelids.

The left top berth was empty. The teenager in the right top berth tried to remember in full detail the way the body of the woman beneath him had moved when she had climbed into the right middle berth. He shifted his hips to take the lump in his jeans out of all possible lines of sight, hiding it completely from those who shared his train compartment. He was tired, but he couldn't sleep.

—

The man in the left middle berth finished his drink and opened
the magazine, which was about the important kinds of national
politics. He got a few pages in and had a little epiphany: the
whole undertaking was just an in-talk record of money and
goods moving from place to place. He was holding an illustrated
shipping manifest. He paged around, each piece reinforcing
his observation, and poured himself another small drink. The
boy in the right top berth thought that if he could just rub his
body lightly against that of the woman who slept in the bunk
beneath him, not really with the intent to touch her but so as to
collect the thin film of sleep that covered her, if he could do that
then he would really sleep, sleep so hard that he would wake up
disoriented and new.

The woman in the right middle berth dreamt that the left
top berth ticket had been bought by a sculptor who had then
been refused the right to travel, and that the bunk held a
foul-smelling empty space in the shape of the sculptor's foul-
smelling (because he smoked, and bathed rarely because he had
no hot water in his flat) body. The real foul-smelling body, she
dreamed, sweated and writhed in the prison of the south. The
man in the left lower berth's heart quit all of a sudden. His wife
heard it and leaned out into the aisle and yelled (as he died he
had turned his good dead ear away from her, so she had to raise
her voice a bit into his bad dead ear) "You can't use a hammer
on that! You need a mallet!" and his whole body clenched with
distaste and his heart fell into its old rhythm.

The boy in the right top berth tried to convince himself that if he could silently and swiftly penetrate the woman who slept so greedily underneath him, when she climaxed (he had an understanding of sexual pleasure inferior to that of his understanding of the hydrodynamics of sleep) her body would release a powerful wave of energy that would incapacitate them all instantly, and when he awoke days later he would be without sin, acne, self-loathing, responsibility, fear and insufficience. He remembered, he thought, that she was wearing a dress. He was extremely tired. His foot joggled against the bunk rail as if jerked on a string.

The left top berth was an unfertilized womb. The man in the left middle berth poured a drink and pictured his entire life as a lavish 50s musical number, with him as a choreographer and a world of salable items as the dancers. He would arrange them such that they unlocked the face of the earth, and they would dance down into the tropics of magma beneath. The man in the left bottom berth ate a fat nugget of rat poison. His wife said, "You promised me a vacation to the cool north shores after you retired," and he vomited sullenly.

The woman in the right middle berth dreamed that her hand was severed, and another person simultaneously began to develop a tumor in his back. Eventually, she approached him and pressed her stump into the shallow depression where the tumor was beginning to protrude through his skin: there was a feeling of completion and sealing, and she was rooted inside

3

him like a dummy's ventriloquist, except that her hand was curled around his vena cava and she could neither control him nor release him.

The woman in the right middle berth's hand clenched into a fist. The boy in the right top berth thought, if she wasn't absolutely necessary for me to sleep, I would slap her in the face for what she does to me. The man in the left middle berth couldn't imagine what could possibly be waiting for him at the center of the earth and had a drink instead. The man in the left bottom berth died and the woman in the right bottom berth started to wail so loud it could wake the dead.

The left top berth was heading north. It was tired of being empty in the south. It huddled into itself and was drawn along in the long trail of car after car.

PARABLE OF THE FORMLESS LORD

Regardless of how she felt about it, Anne's growth precisely recapitulated the process of evolution that had resulted in the lineage that produced Anne. She started as her ancestor, the eukaryote, grew through tadpole to lizard to little mammal— this all happened so quickly—then the small apes, then the bigger one. At menarche, she met herself: Anne the life and Anne the inheritor of generation upon generation of lives. For a minute, they moved in one another, they drained the same blood. After the breeding, Anne's clan was handed down, and Anne's life moved into later days. She became smaller, mind and skin more densely wrinkled, as our descendants will be, slow-moving, wise, quite peaceable, the fixed axle of a wheel around which work revolves. Soon Anne was brought food and drink by servants like a grey queen bee. Years later, they put steel in her hip and a tiny computer in her chest, and then a great many more machines until it was not clear where the person stopped and the rest began.

After that she became non-human; after that she leaned back from time, which had long been a glass against which she had instinctively pressed her face; after that she surrendered her gender; after that we must see her from the posture of worship; after that lights in the sky; after that the source of all power and grief, because we are all crude tools in the hand of the formless lord of our necessary future.

PARABLE OF LOCKDOWN

The children were meek behind my makeshift barricade: an active shooter pushed his way in anyway. He Ramboed right up to me, little beady crazy eyes darting all over my face like a tongue. Did you know, he said, that I am not coping well with various exigencies. I know, I said. Running into you on the street is like getting a speck of dirt in the eye. The children milled.

Another one booted in a few minutes later with a very American-looking contraption that uses unleaded premium to spray thousands of shotgun blasts per second, if you would only give in to your impulse to caress its enormous, jutting trigger. He pointed the barrel at me. Been wronged, he muttered. I nodded even though it was obviously not true. He gestured at the children with the barrel in a way that made me pee. Perform justices, he said. I lined the children up according to their spiritual cleanliness, and I praised or criticized or smacked each one according to arbitrary and extemporaneous impressions. Is it fair, he said. Yes, I said, it is totally fair, I would absolutely never allow even a tiny inaccuracy to sneak into our great and objective system. He handed me his weapon and stood at the end of the line, eyes closed, jaw clenched. Go ahead, he said. It's my turn.

A third one came in panting, flushed with exertion and exhilaration, and hid behind the door while he reloaded each of the thirty-five guns he was carrying. This is the greatest, he said, game I have ever played. Like a video game, I asked, he said no, those are meditations. This is the game of newspapers. I shuffled back, because newspapers don't distinguish allies and enemies; relax, he said, I'm a high scorer. No reason to waste bullets on people who aren't government employees: I'm past civilians. I didn't relax. The next day, the newspaper read DEVIL'S DAY: SOUL-EVISCERATING MADMAN SENDS INNOCENT TOWN SCREAMING TO THE BRINK OF ANNIHILATION.

We were in lockdown and the children were singing their lockdown song. A radio crackled somewhere and an active shooter burst through the door with the kind of tactical nuclear missile that you can buy at gas stations in Missouri. Little red dots from laser sights crisscrossed the room, searching out his body, his melon head, his pockmarked face. He cowered. He hissed, can you tell me real quick I only have a minute can you tell me what a pussy tastes like. I said, nothing special. He said you are god damned wrong it is very very special it is the most special and precious thing and they lit him up.

I was in lockdown and I was making a bonfire of the children to keep warm. The shooter was extremely active, he was wearing himself out. It reminded me of soccer practice, when you make the players drill and drill, pushing them just a little further every day because you don't have any idea what is appropriate or what is sufficient. They spindle and they heave and they become ropy, enraged at the ball, excessive in their off hours. You charge them, they pay: then, sometimes, the other team doesn't show up to the big game, and they look up at you with exhausted mooneyes.

The next shooter dropped down through the foamboard of the ceiling, which is just ersatz, it hides the ducts. He came down right in the middle of the children, and I couldn't tell who was who, but then yes, the only one with the bullet-spitting statue of a pit bull. A moment later an abused toddler with a shoulder-mounted chainsaw launcher kicked in the door, and a laid-off security guard with an armful of anti-personnel mines swung in through the window. The shooters circled like maypole dancers; I smelled sex in the room. The whole thing started to seem totally without narrative, completely unvideoable, which made me fear for the livelihoods of the news crews. A shirt hit the ground: the children clapped and oohed. One hot second later, the PA crackled into life: the lockdown was lifted. Everyone was instructed to go back to their normal business, but we were assuredly at it already.

PARABLE OF HOT GOBS

When the funeral simultaneously crested in terms of emotional intensity and absolute, silent paralysis, I was sent outside to play with a cousin who I had never met before. We went directly into culverts, runoff streams, the concrete foundations of houses that were never built. He was a little snot-nosed intellectual and I was a little snot-nosed intellectual, we were theorizing about worms, the meals they made of corpses, that the ground beneath us was a broad and distributed network of the brain and heart matter of our forefathers. We were working out the cannibal's creed: you eat it, you obtain it. I didn't know whose son he was, I didn't know he was the son of worms.

I have continued this kind of theorizing ever since. When a person dies, at that very moment, they are interacting with an uncountably large number of tiny particles, and into each one they impart a certain amount of information—a shift in spin, trajectory, velocity. With a sufficiently powerful virtual model of the present moment, we could read these tiny bits of information, then work backwards until the dead body leapt into a half-slump, then unexhaled its exhalation, then looked around, racked with pain. This is an outgrowth of the cannibal theory of worms: everything that bounces off us becomes part of us.

I have a second theory that is new, it is that if one could instantaneously transport one's self a galaxy-spanning distance away, and then construct a massive, high-resolution telescope, one could observe the light of those who have passed away, could see directly into the events of the past, the man in his trenchcoat losing his footing on the ice and his outstretched hands missing their grab at the rail, putting them in no good place to protect his long-gone head. I look back on the boys in the culvert like this. I see them, and I can't do anything for them.

We considered the issue for a half hour, perhaps, but our lack of results was frustrating: no matter what we thought, nothing actually happened. Then we gave up bought sodas and hot dogs at the gas station next to the overpass. The sweet and savory, the meat and the fluid made our mouths water long after we'd consumed them, as if we were brimming with some kind of scum-lively spring water, and it was too much for our little bodies to restrain. I had my first fuck-all-of-this feeling and my cousin was about ready to explode, so we hung over the edge of the overpass and spat hot gobs down on the motorists below. They passed beneath us, unaware, in a rhythm that produced the illusion of endlessness.

PARABLE FROM VALVRAVE THE LIBERATOR

Amoral genius L-Elf straddles his opponent and starts to punch him rhythmically in the face. They are both in space suits and it is impossible for L-Elf to harm his adversary, but he punches anyway, left, right, left. They are stranded together on an asteroid, or maybe the moon, and their air is running out: they have precisely the same amount of air. While he thumps the glass faceplate, L-Elf has a terrifically long and involved thought about who he loves and who loves him, why he does the things he does, and whether or not he should press on in his many amoral genius undertakings. None of this has much to do with pounding the man underneath him: he hammers away with gusto. There is a robot fist impaled into the moon's crust near them. They have no plan or opportunity to escape the tiny gravity that holds them down. L-Elf drops machinelike blow after thudding blow, he thinks about a girl he liked once, she wore her hair long.

The foregoing is the realist part of the show, the segment in which we are given endlessly recognizable allegorical versions of ourselves. After the anime establishes our basic unloneliness— we are each trapped on different asteroids with different adversaries, but we are all trapped on asteroids—we are treated to the fan service that keeps viewers coming back week after week. The same fantasy that always occurs recurs: someone speaks the right words, there is a burst of green light, and the spell propels us all towards another rock where we will pound

PARABLE OF THE ROTARY PHONE

I found myself at a summer camp for the scions of upper-middle-crust Houston Texas. During the day, we alternated between violence and Jesus: archery in the morning, then a break for lunch while devotional rock played on the PA, then skeet shooting or lacrosse in the afternoon. Some evenings, we would smear our faces with mud and skulk through the forest to defend or obtain flags; others would feature a film about faith, and the older campers would grab and fondle each other ecstatically in the dim light of Christ's love. These experiences were meant to come together during the rock climbing excursion, where we would master the jagged and unfeeling skin of the earth itself in order to experience an early-morning sermon at the pinnacle.

It was explained to me that the guide rope, the one that arrowed straight down the cliff face, was the teaching of Christ. It was straight and the absolute truth. If you climbed along it without deviation, you might fall, but you'd never fall far—your trust in the Lord and your belayer, your faith community, would catch you. If you ignored it, well, the counselor knifed up his shoulders a little bit and looked at a spot a few degrees above the horizon as if to say *in that case I'll be doing something else, because I won't want to be present for your unavoidable and well-deserved suffering.* I made it about three-quarters of the way up before I heard the buzzing: the guide line was laid directly, almost gingerly, over a wasp's nest. I went as far out to the left as I could to get around it, and when I got to the top, I got a talking to. It went on to the extent that I realized that the counselors had been given a strong and powerful injunction against directly saying that any of our actions as campers had offended or disappointed Jesus; I realized this because every euphemism for such was trotted slowly past me. As a Christian myself and a child, I would normally have been turned into a sobbing wreck by just the hint of my part in the sufferings on Calvary, but as a fatherless child, I was fixated on proving the existence of the wasp's nest, and I didn't notice the evidence of my moral decline until later.

At the crest of the sermon on the crest of the hilltop, the camp organizer held up an old rotary telephone. He unscrewed the mouthpiece, detached the wiring inside, took the face off, the little card with the numbers on it, and opened up the base, letting components spill out. He put the whole mess into a big Ziploc bag and he started shaking it. "Now, some people," he said flatly, "think that if you shake this bag long enough, you're going to get a working telephone by random chance. Does that seem right to you? Look at all this —" and with his non bag-shaking hand he indicated all the Arkansas around us, the white clapboard cross, the trees that kept the riverbank firm and the ones sucking slowly down into the river "— look at yourselves. Does this seem like an accident to you, or does it seem like something that was created for a purpose?" He stopped shaking the bag, but I began to want him to keep shaking it, to shake it harder. I wanted to grab him and shake him until he died and was replaced by someone who was even better at shaking the bag. I didn't care if we got a phone out of it or not. The air was cool, it was that brief part of a hot day where the breeze is light and variable, and the hair on my arms stood up. I felt an invisible set of hands grabbing me by the shoulders, their fingers clenching. I felt my body moving back and forth slowly to the beat of my own pulse.

PARABLE OF THE SIZE OF DOGS

Extremely small dogs take everything exactly as seriously as dogs of other sizes. They struggle just as hard to get good food in large quantity; they bark like they are tearing the world from its hinges; they are equally put out when you prevent them from urinating in a favored location. It is not that they do not know they are small—I once saw a miniature Boston Terrier throw itself off a steep embankment to avoid a passing collie. It is that there is something in the spirit of life which does not adjust to scale.

Extremely small dogs in the White House stalk the curtains and remain annoyingly underfoot during discussions of the most important matters of state. Extremely small dogs in outer space will not brook the invasion of other extremely small dogs into the region of space that they consider to be their own. Extremely small dogs on the time-slowed lip of a black hole will whine and cry for their masters. Extremely small dogs in the pulsing heart of creation will put their butts flat on the carpet and drag themselves forward with their front paws in an attempt to express their anal glands.

The exception to all the above is the depths of the rage of the extremely small dog. It is violence that satisfies rage: destruction is evidence of the importance of the enraged beast. And small dogs cannot destroy, so their rage mounts endlessly. I have seen toy poodles with their jaws clamped down on pant cuffs shake them back and forth so hard that they self-inflict injuries to the spine. I have seen chihuahuas attempt to invent new dark arts in order to smite their foes, but their attempts are always in vain. There is a physical law hidden in the anger of these dogs: all life takes itself equally seriously, but not all life is taken equally seriously. The great luminous animals at the centers of suns have no need to lash out, because they could cause great disruptions by simply drifting off to sleep and going dark. The amoeba sprays acid at anything it touches because hey, fuck everything.

Therefore, when you meet an extremely small dog laying out on a hill as dusk falls and the stars come out, and the dog asks if you've ever really considered how small we are in the grand scheme of things, be on your guard. No dog of any size ever really considers how small it is in the grand scheme of things. All dogs believe themselves to be of sufficiently crucial size. What that dog is saying is *isn't it unfair that I am not bigger* and *don't I seem bigger than this* and *what is so great about the placid, uninvolved light of the spheres*. The musing dog is twisting itself up, fluffing its fur in an attempt to make itself seem larger. It's about to take something from you. It's giving its justification in advance.

PARABLE OF THE GREATCOAT

Okay, so the coat got holes and the holes got large and then the coat was holes. This seems like the whole story but it is just a part of the story that you, one day, will be forced to think past. In the distant future, when you consider the coat, you'll have to immediately, without reference to its now-irretrievable clothness, consider it as a long-since sprouted farm for holes. The skewed balance of its brief life in cloth as compared to its endless existence as a post-coat will, to you, represent the coat. This extinguished quality will source all answers to all questions about the coat: what is its value? How does it make you feel? What is the good of the coat? Were you to be handed a precise replica of the garment, you would be unable to see anything but its nascent rips and tears.

Once you have internalized this attitude, perhaps slept on it or dreamed on it, go through the above paragraph and replace "the coat" with the personal name of a parent, spouse, or intimate friend, and replace the word "cloth" with the word "flesh." The holes stay holes. Now how do you feel about "the coat"? How does it feel to bury your face in the cloth of the coat? How much should you have paid for the coat, so long ago when you were first desiring it? What are you going to do to stay warm, now that you know that all coats are full of, are mostly, are bursting with the lack of their cloth?

PARABLE OF MUSIC

The musician Pink had a fight with one of her friends, somebody she had been taking hard drugs with and had come to suspect was a less than positive, supportive influence. So she wrote a song: the chorus was *I swear you're just like a pill / instead of making me better / you're making me ill*. She recorded it, it sounded great, A&R loved it, and it hit #8 on the Hot 100. Pink was greatly pleased. Teenagers everywhere, implicitly or explicitly, reexamined their attachment to their friends; for most it was just a fleeting thought, but millions of people connected the "you" of the song to a flesh-and-blood "you." A woman in Shrevesport who believed deeply in omens dropped her oxycontin-dealing boyfriend just days before they would have conceived their first child. Another woman, in International Falls, North Dakota, listened to it on repeat as she worked up the courage to pop apart a perfectly serviceable marriage, and then her son listened to it in his room, visualizing the humiliation, apology and return of his mother. A man heard a snatch of the song from a passing car (everyone had heard it once by now, more or less, so he only needed to hear a note or two to access the song's central concept) and promised himself he would lay off the whiskey, then almost immediately broke that promise. A thirteen-year old girl docked her iPod and played the song and writhed around on her bed in bra and panties on webcam, and the resulting video was scrubbed from the internet forever by vigilant webmasters; another girl of the same age did the same thing in slightly lower light and her clip was used to advertise pornographic websites for years to come. A retired engineer caused a three-car accident while trying to switch the radio away from "Just Like a Pill"; the sound of it playing while he was pinned by the dashboard recurs to him, and he feels nauseous, hallucinatory when he comes across it now.

Pink sits crosslegged in a big house in the Hollywood Hills, sorting through seventies power ballads. She sits at the hub of the spokes of the great wheel which turns us all, but is herself motionless, drinking a bottle of coconut water. She is not absent, and she is not unaffected; she is not responsible, and she is not uninvolved. She works hard to stay fit and she writes music that makes her feel pleased with herself. She lets the rest go: this is the ideology held by gods. The act of making is not as complex as we pretend it is, and what we fantasize is the control wielded by the prime mover of all things is, in reality, something ephemeral, unpredictable, a flutter or pop.

PARABLE OF CASHIERS

When I was two years old, what I could offer retail clerks was
entree to a borderless realm of perfectly legitimate desire. You
could sit behind the counter and visualize pulping the melon of
my whining head; you could reach out when my parents weren't
looking and pat my soft sweaty hair, you could make whatever
faces, odd faces, faces that later you'd realize came directly from
the events of your life, nightmare faces and faces blown up into
huge self-important versions of themselves.

By the time I turned seventeen, what I gave to the people at the
checkout was my own unrequitable ardor. I had never been with
a service employee before, or in truth with anybody, it could be
you, is that what you're thinking right now? And how about
now. My eyes flat and open on whoever you are. Perhaps after I
am with you, or the friend to whom you introduce me, or your
sibling or parent, after I have been loved, we will all laugh about
the way I nervously started and stopped the grocery conveyor
belt by blocking the tiny laser with my thumb.

When I was thirty-five I had a slouchy needless experienced
humanism, and I could give that to cashiers of all kinds. It is a
kind of letting go: sure, I want to buy four identical wrinkle-free
shirts, if you ring them up for me I can get even closer to doing
my laundry on a two-month cycle. But if you don't, and I can
think of a dozen reasons why you wouldn't, I don't give a fuck,
I'll go to some other store or just quit and iron more or spend

more at the cleaners. I mean, I am not even here. You're here, that's important, that's good. Let's let you take the field for a while: I am tired, nothing would please me more than for you to be you for a while, and I'll just mope along in your wake.

At this rate I can make a prediction about what I will be able to offer service personnel by the time I reach sixty. They will reach the end of the line, bag the last items, and there will be a pause. They'll announce that the register is open, as they've been instructed to do, but nobody will arrive. The customer timer at their station will deactivate; they will take a clean, slow breath that is free of me and everything I was or could have been. It will be possible to taste the spices of the daily air: sweetness, repose, and empty, submissive possibility.

PARABLE OF THE KLS

He was at church. They were shaking water on him and yelping and he couldn't breathe or think. He knew something was supposed to happen to his soul, a pinching and bursting that they were both attempting to cause and claiming could not be caused by external forces. Someone started to play the guitar and the words of the hymn floated over to him, unintelligible, and the code and the suffer of it all was just too much, so he curled up on the floor and hopelessly produced the Kentucky Lonesome Sound. The crowd erupted in cheers; they robed him in white, they started calling him brother.

When they finally captured one of the alien battle robots, intact and operational, it took days to figure out how to crack the carapace, and then many more days to delicately separate the mesh of bioelectric wiring that rippled like a musculature under the hard exterior. Inside was an oblong vault of chalk; inside that was the hint of a sphere, drawn in thin, curved surfaces of steam; inside that was the Kentucky Lonesome Sound.

I have been known to drink too deeply from the Kentucky Lonesome Sound. I look down at my knees, which come to look like images of distant and inanimate objects. My fingers tremble and jitter as I remember a very few things with what seems like rare clarity. This is actually the effect of forgetting almost everything else: at some point the experience is only and purely singular, all else is crowded out, my crimes, my consciousness, your worried hand on my faithless arm. It is like floating in lakewater at dusk, considering the possibility that you'll never swim back? Like the heavy way your arms and legs go numb when you finally, finally, are tired enough to fall asleep in the back of a moving pickup? I can't remember.

Once in a dream I was your mother, and you were a teenager, and we were having a screaming argument about the Kentucky Lonesome Sound. You said *it loves me*, but with a kind of whine in your voice, *it lohves me*, and I told you it would never do anything but hurt you, that its butterfly knife and ditchweed dimebags were the first step on a long, precipitous fall from grace, but you told me grace was for assholes and slammed out the door, and I was so sad for you and so proud, like when you were a baby and the soft fragrant patch on your head knitted and closed into thin, protective skull.

I dream of a political candidate who was once admitted suicidal to a mental hospital, there to languish and smoke, and upon release had made a complex estimation that if judiciously pursued, television and masturbation and medication was preferable to the great screaming crush of the heavens. He would then have expanded this deal to include newspaper-reading, and then the study of law, and then the representation of people like himself, which is all people. At the end of every day he would carefully total the balance and make sure everything was still worth it, and check the math, and plan the next day according to what he could afford. When he arrives

at the great rostrum of national attention, and makes the
Kentucky Lonesome Sound, the people will finally wake and
move.

It's simply not possible to train a dog to make any of the
Lonesome Sounds, regardless of their state of origin. When a
dog howls, it howls for somebody: it cannot ever howl because
of the lack of anybody. Coyotes can learn with effort; birds
never do. You can train a person with great ease: just put them
in the box. I know you know what kind of box I'm talking
about, don't be a hypocrite, you use it all the time. You work in a
factory for jails.

You ask me sometimes whether I love you or not. You can
tell when I do because I will not be making the Kentucky
Lonesome Sound. This does not mean that I am not lonesome;
even a bed with you in it is a rut at the roadside, a long tussle
with bad weather, a father with a habit to wander. It means
that I am suppressing it, layer of steam, layer of chalk, so you
can have your turn. That I am standing at the edge of the dark,
listening to the music of your own abandoned and profitless
mine.

PARABLE OF HANGNAIL

Don't you want to bite it out?

Don't you want to bite it out?

Don't you want to bite it out?

Don't you want to bite it out?

PARABLE OF CHARISMA OR VIRTUE

If you die, and your lifelong partner feels terrible grief, such
that the simple fried rice she makes for herself when she needs
to be comforted looks all of a sudden like a pile of harsh grain,
and she pours a glass of acid-smelling wine and talks to her
mother, who seems all of a sudden to be unsympathetic, even
uncomprehending, such that she cannot even sleep because she
can no longer appreciate the satisfaction of sinking into the
dark couch where we repudiate ourselves, if she starts chewing
long strips of skin off of the inside of her lip, then the question
is not yet settled.

If you die and her pain recedes, as it does, gradually, leaving an
open space, and she is well enough that she makes an attempt
to fill that open space with something that is not you or the
memory of you, then the question is not yet settled.

If she forgets you, the question remains unsettled.

If what she does to fill the particular space you left is take up
boating, pushing a sturdy canoe out onto the beautiful lakes
of her childhood, reveling in the dapple of the water, the wood
ducks dropping into the dapple at the terminus of their end-
of-day arc, if she sits out there floating and feels a whole-body
pleasure from the touch of the wind and the smell of warm
mud and the sound of dragonflies, if she wonders why she spent
so much time out in the world contesting everything and

PARABLE OF THE MINISKIRT WITH HEART-SHAPED FRONT POCKETS

Here are my genitals, no, wait, my feelings. Actually: here is my denim. What I've got in my pockets could be cold, surprisingly stiff, or empty or anything: *look at the denim* is a performative act expressly and only intended to provoke denim-looking, and you are not and never have been its target, at least not like I am. When my eyecrotchheart circulates, my skirted sisters are the best adjuncts to myself as they appreciate it or sniff at it in condescension. So do not pollute my self-regard by looking directly into the denim: I would like a moment alone to spend with my garment. Oh weird love skirt, make me love and weird. Because I am lonely, and I have heard in the news that the bones of normal people positively litter the ground.

PARABLE OF THE TRIP

The hippie waiter unholstered his Windex and told the busboy, see now cleaning glass is like you got to do it completely, when it's done it's a trip, it's not even there, you can't see it. But it is there. Am I right? The waiter seemed genuinely to want the answer. The busboy leaned over and tried to look at a piece of perfectly cleaned glass: form without border, mass without weight, light without heat. His forehead felt damp.

Later the busboy traveled compulsively, as if trying to wipe off the city of his origin. In Brussels, he encountered a person of basically indiscriminate gender, dressed in local fashion, who was wholly capable in Dutch, French and English, to the extent that he could not figure out where s/he was from. He soon forgot the experience—but the person was Spanish and had grown up in a slow-rolling kind of domestic crematorium, it had scraped off all the identifying marks. They moved perpendicular to one another and never met again.

The busboy began to teach students. He tried to teach them to visualize and analyze their own culture, the womb in which they had been raised, but he never told them that what he really wanted was a side effect of this: to obliterate the self's culture, to make all of them less contingent upon context, less determined. He would point at them when they talked about the power of choice and hiss, individualism? You are an American boy! Insinuating that such is a ball on a chain.

When the busboy died, at the funeral half of the audience spent the ceremony thinking, who was that man really? The other half were the elderly who had grown up in the old industries, the workers of the age of service. While they mourned they took whatever drugs they'd been able to afford and the drugs entered them and, in time, became indistinguishable from the rest of them.

PARABLE OF STONE CLOTHES

Before, as it turned out, the fire ships came, before the alien saucers turned all oxygen to flame, I swam through non-traditional air to get you gum and Coke. I had a feeling of horizontal, outward-pulling tension in my trunk, like hands tugging my ribs open, but I was completely used to it. I thought it was humid and that I was still a little drunk from the day before; the thickness of the air was in fact an unexploded aerosol, something they'd been pumping down for days behind their uncanny scrim.

You wanted the Coke because you wanted it. You didn't want the gum, but I was getting myself a Coke too, and I wanted you to have more than me, you know? Because I needed so much from you.

As it turns out, the lava sky clothed us igneously anyway. None of our scores ever got settled up; the tallies and chits lay senescent under a half-inch of ash. As it turns out, though, if I ever find out about who did what to who and how much, I will neither apologize nor expect penitence from you. Because the one fire broke over my body and my family and my enemies in a single, socialist, annihilating wave, and for the first time I could really tell where the doors of the treasure-house ended and the broken field of worthless totems began.

PARABLE OF TEMPORARY LODGING

Hotels are sexy. Search online for incidents of illicit semi-public or public exposure of the nude human body, and they will disproportionately take place in the hallways of hotels. A motel is even sexier; an hourly motel sexier yet. At the Coral Court Motel in Missouri, where I once dreamed of taking you but no longer do, they had enclosed garages, which means that you could drive in, have all manner of momentary entertainment, and slip out without this period of time infringing upon or narratively linking itself to the span of the rest of your life. That's a moment: what crouches inside a separation, the meat between little walls. The flower of youth is a pay-first road motel. Your youth, used up on whatever, spent on this poem. Real flowers are even lustier, even more dissipated. There is no hotel sexier than the swelling and bursting of mayflies. If you really want sex, though, think: the time of the radical deformation of a cannonball striking a stone wall, the tininess of your whole lineage in regards to the age of stars, the moment a photon boils into radiant heat. Come to me compromised. The photon experiences, then exits a perverse brand of time dilation; the atoms it excites slow down, but their response doesn't last long.

PARABLE OF OLD SWEDES

The upright elderly clustered around the supine elderly, they were all Swedes, they smelled like their alchemical kitchens, smoked meat and urine and smear of lard. I don't know why I was there, but that sensation is near-constant. I was born from *gather ye rosebuds*. I was born in a hammock on William Duffy's farm. These people were far from me on each possible axis, x (mouth distance), y (snow distance), z (toughness distance). They could therefore only be metaphors, distant little horizon metaphor dots, and obediently they moved with the jerking grace of metaphor and leaned over the dying man with the inexorability of metaphor. They knew it would come to this both in fact and in my conception of fact, which is to say that we were starting to have the togetherness of metaphor as well. The dying man had seemingly every blockage, I wanted to reach down his throat and scoop the mucus out, but it was clear that the burble was way down in there, now, and nothing to do about it.

The elderly Swedes just watched. They put their jerky hands, their pee hands, their Crisco hands on the man who laid down. They were talking in a language I didn't understand, but there was a pattern in it and so I had to accept that it was real. Then they were talking in a language that I did understand, they were looking right at me and waving their frondlike lips, but there was no pattern in it and it felt dreamlike. They wanted towels or sheets or something made of fabric. They wanted living water in great quantities, or if that was unavailable they wanted stilled snowwater or bitter water which I had survived drinking or water from which I had cast the demons out. If there was no water I was to rub leaf-fragrant dirt into their skin. This took years to understand, probably I have invented it, regardless they looked directly at me and made such requests as they could.

The man on his back made the bow of the keel of a ship, as if snapping back to his natural shape. I leaned in unconsciously, and a man in a low hat and a fury of white hair turned to block my approach. He spread out his hands as if casting two fistfuls of dice. He said "You are only for the provision of waters or dirts." Part of his translation problem was that all my generosity came from the sensation that I had never given anything to anyone. "Stand back," he said. The disc of the old man's hat was perfectly still and the circumference was parallel to the floor. He said, "we give to him the air."

PARABLE OF THE BIRTH OF ZHUANGZI

My wife was going to have a baby and the baby died and the baby was born anyway and the baby was a very small Zhuangzi. He was not a baby, he was a fetus, not a fetus, an embryo, he was a curl, he was a gray smudge between concept and execution, a feather fallen loose from the arrow of progress. He said, I'm telling you. Animal life is a limited life and the world is an unlimited world, the world despises your animal life, it's swallowing your little chimp life whole. Zhuangzi had died because he was made of incomplete genetic information, or perhaps because all our bodies are singing with poison. My wife tried to love Zhuangzi because he was her son but he brushed her off. He wanted me to promise him that I would leave home immediately and with such theatrics that no home could reassert itself in the place where I'd left it. He kept gesturing at his own gelatinousness, he said this is not natural, you made it all up, he said let's throw off the oppression of descent. I knew he was a real person and that he was my own real son because he was so incredibly scared about having died. He said to have a party after he was gone, he said never to say anything about him to anyone so that the unspoken word of him would remain eternally identical to itself, the pregnancy of the silence before speech. He said he was just a dream of himself anyway, that none of it mattered. I told him everything would be okay. I tried to name him something guttural and unwritable, but he had already gone back to not ever really having been here.

PARABLE OF HOW TO CUT THE MEAT

Before you even attend to these instructions, you have already thrust your knife into the carcass. This is your way, and let us assume it to be unimpeachable. Stab it in there. Think about your adolescence: as soon as you knew what wrong was, you had already done wrong.

Wander the knifepoint through the theme park of the animal. Flesh is of and for children, the endless row of skee-ball games at the midway: it is the same to itself, a fascinant in every iteration, it spits tickets redeemable for essentially nothing, but you can walk up and down the rows all day, watching the lights, listing under the force of their looping music. You play with it because it was made to induce your play.

Carve whatever messages you like into the dead body. I have said it to you, and I say it to you again, and still you do not understand it, and still even I do not act as if it is true: dude. Dude. Nobody is listening. Just go nuts in there, let your arms speak freely.

What is left, then, should you eat it? Of course not. Dice it up fine, make a mush, and then just wait and watch. This is the origin of the rest of the everything: the fermentation, the infection, the fostering, the foment.

PARABLE OF THE OLD MAN IN THE FIELD

When I was a child my family would tell stories, sing songs, and recite poems to me from memory. Sometimes they would say that the stories were jokes told by their crazy neighbors back in Iowa; sometimes they would say that they were things my father collected during his many travels; sometimes when I asked where it all came from, they would act concerned and tend to me as if I was having a fever dream. As I grew older, I became literate and wily, so I started to write down these stories, at first with no purpose other than the feeling of power it gave me to see them on paper, but later driven by the realization that they described a world that could have been real, something my family participated in that they never shared with me.

The old man was working to know and perfect the end of life, and he had renounced all his worldly goods and moved out to a fallow farm field in order to focus on potential solutions and practices. He was leathery and poor. Once one of his followers—he did have followers, this was the early 1970s and people were still credulous, idealistic—asked him how he paid his taxes and still ended up with enough money to buy tobacco. The old man unbuttoned his work shirt. Over his chest was a single, thick mass of scar, which radiated out at the edges into a dozen knife-tendrils, indicating that his chest had been cracked open and entered again and again. He watched his disciple with the watery/crusty eyes of a salt pond evaporating, looking all the world like the gatekeeper of a portal overgrown with vines.

—

I have to assume that the old man never found anything out, but he did once say this: "A person adheres to the dimensions: xward, yward, zward, endwards in time. The mind adheres as well. Language assumes a location in all things: but one day we surrender our points. We coalesce graceward. We refine inside the girding of the grid. We taut the backbone of the standing wave."

The way that the old man had gotten famous, or at least well-known to the extent that he was, was that one day he drew a map of the earth in the dirt. He walked from one end of his map to the other. He carved some scrap wood into unfamiliar shapes, and placed the carvings on the fenceposts nearest to him. The rumor soon began that he had visited faraway places, and people came to ask for the insights of the people there. One of the carvings was of a flower with an index finger piercing up through the cup of it; one was of a gazelle, but where the horns belonged, two more hooves grew gracefully from the animal's skull.

The old man was awful with money but he loved nickels. If you gave him a nickel, he'd put it between his thumb and middle finger and snap them, ejecting the nickel at high speed. He was very accurate and could raise a welt in a disciple at twenty-five paces; when he did, he'd give a sudden, barking laugh. There was a time of day in the field at which all the cast-off nickels in varying stages of tarnish would catch the setting sun, creating a kind of brutal, irregular starscape.

There was a song, too, but I don't know the relationship of the song to the rest: it could have been an elaborate joke, my people truly enjoy long-term comedy. I only remember the last verse, but it went like this: *It's decoration day. Tear bright plants from the earth. Sway wild, spray the pollen and the seed. People, are you having a good time now? Just like the flowers that come in May?*

The old man became extremely ill, and he instructed his followers to go out into the world and collect the utterances of men and women who were right in the midst of dying, to ask them to describe their experience just as it was happening to them. His followers, who were believers but retained their Midwestern reserve, agreed not to bother any of the afflicted, and instead wrote fictitious "Notes from the Dead" in order to appease him in his last days. He was, as the story goes, satisfied, and his satisfaction did much to recommend him as a true prophet rather than one who struggled and failed.

On behalf of their master, the disciples sacrificed the question *how can it be known* for an experience of death; on my behalf, my family has made it impossible for me to distinguish my thoughts about dying from layered epistemological puzzles. Was there an old man and a field? Were the stories faithful— were they things the old man had said and done? Could quiet thought ever be enough for anyone to achieve an understanding of the world after our world? Were my brothers and sisters telling me something by describing the old man's willingness to accept fantasies? How can I ever know what they were trying to tell me, considering their gingerness towards me, the way they pat me dry like a beading wound, their funerary care?

PARABLE OF PERSISTENT EMAIL

Nobody speaks to their ancestors any more, and you are not famous. Once you die, praying to you will be a waste of time, and you know this and those that know you know this. So the last address addressed to you will be a spam email generator, left running and forgotten. Estonia or the Czech Republic will see a dramatic uptick in its economic health: the spammers will open internet service providers and buy equipment by the ton. The penis-mercantile architecture with which they generated their seed money will persist, eagerly plunging itself into your numb account, the drive of them dwarfed by the power of the new body in which they float. Or a person will send some spam, go broke, and sell their list of names, then the seller will sell, then the seller's buyer will sell, and your own holy handle will be handed down to generation upon generation of skinny, chain-smoking teens. The come-on will remain recognizably unimaginable: *EXTEND YOUR PASSION into a NO-COST PRESIDENTIAL ARBITRAGE: local bi±coinz are waiting for you to HOPE ALL OVER THEM.* They expect you not to answer, so they are never surprised when you don't.

I'm not ashamed that I dream of you reading this mail, although I know you won't, and I know you wouldn't if you could. That's okay, this isn't your dream. I visualize you crawling through the folder with this transcendental, angelic patience, until you get all the way back to the years immediately after your death, right when people stopped dreaming about you.

THE PARABLE OF CERTAIN VIDEO GAMES

There is a type of game on the internet called Tower Defense: you are the master of a castle or town which a twisting road approaches. Unending processions of monsters called creeps walk toward the castle, and you build towers full of archers to shoot arrows at the creeps. The more you kill, the more gold you earn, and you spend it on more towers and more archers. As time progresses, the creeps get stronger, more numerous, thirstier for blood, and the defense must be more frantic, the arrows thicker and sharper, costlier. Eventually and no matter what, they break through the defenses: they fall on the city in wave after dark wave, their mandibles crunching bone, leaving nothing but razed and salted earth in their wake. Still, though, it always seems like they earn their meal when they breach your elaborate defenses, and in any event after minutes of furious clicking, you're hardly ever sad to see the city go.

There is also a tradition of games in which certain events— say, killing several of something you do not understand very quickly, before you have time to think about it—earn you an achievement or medal. This produces a kind of nested victory that motivates you to play the game again and again in order to accumulate medals, which range from the simple to the baroque and unlikely. Almost universally, the final medal, past which no more game exists, is a reward for winning all the other medals, but is itself identical to all the other medals, and gives no special power or honor that is not staid and incremental.

Long ago, games pretended to be eternal. Past your skill, there always seemed to be an infinite amount more game: if you were perfectly good, you could play forever. In Pac-Man, though, when you get to the 256th board, it is half-occluded by a jumble of gibberish, and those who want to pass through it must play blind. They say that there is no way to complete the kill screen. They say that one man has done it, but that he is a liar. They say that after the kill screen, the whole game begins again, except that the ghosts never dematerialize. They say that the kill screen is made by the program attempting to draw hundreds of pieces of fruit, one on top of the other, into the hidden pixels beneath the game cabinet, on top of the closed maze: strawberries, grapes, peaches, cherries, eight keys eight times repeated, apples, aliens, a pair of bells.

ACKNOWLEDGMENTS

Many thanks to the journals in which these pieces first appeared:

Berkeley Poetry Review: "Parable of Old Swedes"

Inch: "Parable of the Rotary Phone," reprinted in the *Best Small Fictions 2017* from Braddock Avenue Books.

Queen Mob's Teahouse: "Parable of Lockdown"

Sou'wester: "Parable of the North Train," "Parable of the Old Man in the Field"

NICK ADMUSSEN teaches Chinese literature at Cornell University. He is the author of four chapbooks, including *Movie Plots* from Epiphany Editions and *The Experiment in Morbidity* from Grey Book Press. He also translates Chinese poetry and is the author of *Recite and Refuse: Contemporary Chinese Prose Poetry*.

❀

COLOPHON

Text is set in a digital version of Jenson, designed by Robert Slimbach in 1996, and based on the work of punchcutter, printer, and publisher Nicolas Jenson. The titles here are in Futura.

✻

NEW MICHIGAN PRESS, based in Tucson, Arizona,
prints poetry and prose chapbooks, especially
work that transcends traditional genre. Together
with DIAGRAM, NMP sponsors a yearly chapbook
competition.

DIAGRAM, a journal of text, art, and schematic,
is published bimonthly at THEDIAGRAM.COM.
Periodic print anthologies are available from the New
Michigan Press at NEWMICHIGANPRESS.COM.